JUST ANOTHER DAY AT THE MORGUE

BL Maxwell

JUST ANOTHER DAY AT THE Morgue

Spirit Boys Series

BL Maxwell

COPYRIGHT

This book identifies product names and services known to be trademarks, registered trademarks, or service marks of their respective holders. The author acknowledges the trademarked status and trademark owners of all products referenced in this work of fiction. The publication and use of these trademarks is not authorized, associated with, or sponsored by the trademark owners.

Warning:

Intended for a mature 18+ audience only. This book contains material that may be offensive to some and is intended for a mature, adult audience. It contains graphic language, explicit sexual content, and adult situations.

one

Bran

I walked the hall of the hospital like I always did, head down with earbuds in, and not looking around as I hurried to my office in the hospital morgue. I'd been here a few weeks now, and every day I wondered why I thought it was a good idea to take a job that was surrounded by so much death. But in a way I was part of death.

Not only in my job as a coroner, but the fact my mother had been a Necromancer. She could call upon any spirit and compel them to do whatever she asked of them. Her ability came from magic, but I had inherited a gift from her that I fought to hide daily, and working here made it even harder to do that.

Buddy leaned in close to my leg and I had to fight the urge to reach down and pet him. He'd died years ago, but my childhood dog had never left me. He seemed to know I needed him and was with me almost constantly. His whimper of warning had me looking up and as soon as my eyes were on the old woman wandering down the hall she was in my face yelling.

"Do you see me? Can you hear me? Help me. I don't know where I'm at."

I forced myself not to react and walked through her. The cold that ripped through my body was horrible, and the images I gained from it were not much better. Hurrying to the morgue, I slammed the door shut and slumped against it.

"Tough morning?" Jordan, my assistant asked as he slid the chair out from his desk.

"You wouldn't believe me if I told you," I mumbled. I mumbled a lot around Jordan. Mostly to stop myself from saying something that would make him question my sanity, but also because I really liked him and didn't want him to leave.

"We got a new one," he said as I walked through the door that led to the examination suite. There on the table was a bag that I'd seen many times. Only the body inside was different. Buddy walked over and lay down off to the side like he always did. I still wasn't sure why his spirit had stuck around. Maybe he knew I needed him, or maybe he chose to stay. Either way I was glad he was always there for me.

At the end of the table stood a man. He'd obviously been in an accident. His skull was visible through the gash on his forehead, and his hands were bloody and mangled. He watched me as I walked around the room, but I was careful not to show him I knew he was there.

Then something very strange happened. Buddy walked over to him and sat in front of him. The man reached down and petted him, his hand lingering on Buddy's silky ears as he glanced at me. "You can see me," he whispered.

I forced myself not to react and to concentrate on the clipboard that had been resting on top of the body. It said he'd been in a horrible car accident while driving to Sacramento from Nevada. He had no family, no next of kin. No one to claim the body, and no one to make sure he had a decent burial. I wondered again why Buddy had gone to him. He tended to stay away from other spirits, and I'd often wondered if he couldn't see them, or if he *chose* to ignore them. Either way, with all the spirits we were exposed to daily, this had never happened.

"What's your dog's name," the spirit asked.

"Buddy," I said, an automatic response to a question I hadn't been asked for more than ten years. Buddy grinned his doggy grin at me while enjoying the attention he was getting from the spirit who seemed to be all alone in both life and death. "Do you remember what happened?" I decided to dive right in since he wasn't attacking me or yelling at me *to* help him.

"You can hear me? I thought so, but I don't know how I knew." He looked confused as he stared off into the distance. I turned to look in the direction his eyes were fixed on, but all I saw was the tile wall of the morgue.

"I can. Unfortunately," I admitted, and unzipped the bag. His body was an even bigger mess than his spirit was, and when he saw himself, he gasped, and in an instant, he was standing beside me.

"What happened to me?"

"Blunt force trauma. That's what happens when you don't wear your seatbelt." I finished reading the report, and knew I'd find out far more with the autopsy.

"I always wear my seatbelt. Always," he murmured, and when I glanced up at him, he was looking down at his body. "Is this how it always is?"

"Only when there's unfinished business. Did you have some unfinished business—Justice? That's your name? For real?"

"Jus for short. What unfinished business?" His voice took on the breathy quality that told me he'd be vanishing soon. I wasn't sure if they ran out of energy, or something pulled them somewhere else. Mostly I tried not to talk to them, so there was a lot I didn't know and was unwilling to ask about.

"Only you know that." I slid his body out of the bag. It had extensive damage. The accident he'd been in had to have been horrible, not only was his body mangled but it looked like there'd been a fire. Which explained why half of his head looked the way it did. "Looks like the accident was worse than you thought."

"What was that?" Jordan asked, as he walked in. "Oh, wow. Yeah, that looks like it was a really bad accident." He turned his back to the table and focused on the wall instead. "I just wanted to warn you, they're bringing down one of the patients that didn't make it. She's been on life support for a while now, but her family finally decided to let her go." He still focused on the wall.

"Thanks Jordan, you can go back out to the office if you'd rather." Jordan was very good at his job, but so far, he hadn't gotten used to being around the dead.

"No, it's okay I don't mind." He wrapped his arms around his waist and seemed to force himself to stay where he was. Buddy glided over to him and leaned against him. He took a deep breath and relaxed as much as he could. "I'm sorry. I'm trying to get used to it."

"I understand, it's not for everyone. But you're doing a great job."

"Part of my job is assisting you when you're doing an autopsy." He sounded defeated, but I knew more than anyone how hard this job was.

"How about if I call you once I'm done. Then you can go through his things and see if you find any information about a next of kin."

"I'll be waiting," he said before rushing to the door.

"Well, you tried Buddy." He huffed at me before going back to the spot he liked to lay at and curling up.

TWO
Jordan

I tried to stick it out, but seeing that guy in such a mess was hard for me to stomach. Bran was able to look at every case like the professional he was. Unlike me who felt it all. All their pain, and especially all their sorrow. His spirit dog Buddy leaned heavy on me, trying to siphon off some of the pain and give me some relief, but it wasn't enough. I'd heard Bran say his name on many occasions and worked out the fact Buddy had been his dog, and for some reason, his spirit was still here.

As soon as Bran excused me, I practically ran to my desk, and scrambled to pull out the bag of crystals I kept in the drawer. My hands shook as I took out the large piece of selenite, I would use to store everything I'd absorbed.

After speaking the words that had been passed down in my family for generations, saor mi o'n phian, I started to feel some relief.

The crystal glowed with the power it was now charged with, a power I didn't know how to control, and didn't want to use. Some in my family used the power for good while others chose to use it for bad. But I did my best not to use it at all. Much in the way Bran tried to ignore the fact he could see every spirit that crossed his path.

He didn't need to tell me this, it was obvious in the way he would become distracted and seem to stare off at nothing. My uncle was the same, and over the years it was harder and harder for him to hide it, or to deal with the constant wants and needs of the dead.

"Jordan, can you come in here please?" Bran called from the other room.

I shoved the crystals back in my drawer and braced myself for more. I walked into the room where he now had the deceased on the table and thankfully, he'd covered most of him. I'd seen many bodies in the time I'd worked here, but it never got any easier for me, and it was painful every single time.

Buddy leaned against my leg again, even though I couldn't see him I could feel his warmth. Which was weird since he was a spirit, but he was kind, and that kindness shone through the coldness of death.

"I noticed he had a wallet in his pants can you check for a next of kin?"

"Sure." I walked over to where he'd left his belongings and picked up the wallet. A bolt of cold ran through my arm and I had to force myself not to flinch.

"Are you okay?" Bran asked, looking up from where he was finishing his notes on injuries, and abrasions on the body.

"Yeah, just jumpy today." I knew it was a lame excuse, but if he expected me to not notice him talking to spirits, then I expected him to not question when I reacted to energy I was trying not to react to.

I walked over to where he kept the bins where the belongings were stored. And after putting the clothing in one of them, I opened his wallet to see what I'd find. There were a few credit cards, an ATM card, a coffee rewards card, and a picture of a man next to a motorcycle. "There's no driver's license but there are a few credit cards maybe we can find him from them?"

"Give it a try," Bran said as he got lost in his work.

I hurried back to my desk and googled the name, Justice Rafferty. Not much came up, but there was a Facebook post about someone looking for a man with that same name. It looked like he'd driven to Sacramento from Nevada, but the post didn't say why he'd left or where he was going. They'd been posting on social media hoping someone had seen his truck and could tell them where he was.

There was a picture on the post that was definitely the guy in the other room. He was 34, single, and had not shown up for work over a month ago. The post said he had no reason to leave the state.

"They're going to be surprised that he ended up in Sacramento," I mumbled just as Bran walked through the door.

"Did you find something?" he asked and looked over my shoulder.

"There's someone out of Nevada that's been looking for a coworker that has been missing for around a month. It doesn't sound like he had any connection to the Sacramento area. I'll message them and see if I can find out more information."

After Bran left the room, I took the credit card and held it between my hands. Closing my eyes, I opened my senses hoping to find out more. A shock of pain sliced through my skull, and I fought the urge to vomit. No images came to me. Nothing that would help with his identity other than the post I'd found. It was so frustrating. My power was limited to emotions, and feelings, so unless there were strong emotions attached to an object it was useless to me.

But still I had a niggling feeling there was something more here than a man who had left home and gotten into a traffic accident. I slipped the cards and picture back into the wallet before I noticed another card. It was for a local psychic and had a time and today's date written on it.

I knew the psychic. Janis, she helped a lot of the local ghost hunters and urban explorers with anything from the other side of the realm they didn't know how to deal with. Janis was always willing to help and had more experience than anyone else in the Sacramento area. But why would he have her card?

As I thought about it, the temperature in the room dropped, and I knew a spirit was close by even if I couldn't see it. I tensed up, anticipating what could happen next. Just then Bran burst through the door, he looked up and the blood drained from his face.

"Jordan, don't move," he whispered, and his focus was directly in front of me.

"What is it?" I asked, as I held my breath and tried like hell not to move at all.

"You wouldn't believe me if I told you."

"Try me." His eyes met mine for a split-second before he was focused once again on what was in front of me. Then the pain hit. In an instant Bran was in front of me, so close all I could see was his face. The pain receded, but I wasn't sure why, and I realized I'd closed my eyes. When I opened them again, I was caged in between his body and the wall. He had both his arms outstretched and his hands pressed against the wall. His face was so close I could feel his breath on my lips.

"What's happening?" I asked, then I felt his ghost dog lean against my leg.

"You're going to think I'm crazy, but I can see ghosts, and right now the spirit of the man in there on the table is trying to enter your body. Buddy and I can hold him off for a while but not forever. And he's very determined to get in."

I met his eyes and squared my shoulders. "Then let him." I hadn't done this before, and in fact tried to keep a distance from spirits if I could. But I sensed I needed to help this spirit if I could.

THREE

Bran

His words stunned me. For one thing, he was not shocked at all when I admitted I could see spirits. He also didn't question who Buddy was. "Do you know what you're agreeing to?"

"Yes. I've touched the other side of the veil many times. I think he may have contacted a local psychic, but I don't know why. Maybe he can tell us."

I glanced over my shoulder at the spirit who now stood directly behind me. A moment before he'd been fighting against me to get to Jordan. "I don't think you understand what I'm saying," I whispered.

"He can give us some answers." Jorden met my eyes, and there was a level of understanding there that shocked me.

He knew exactly what was happening. My mind rushed to grapple with the fact we'd worked here together so close to the dead, but nothing like this had happened before.

Buddy was still there, and I forced myself not to look down at him when he leaned harder against Jordan and looked up at me with a whimper. He only did that when he warned me of spirits he seemed to sense I'd want to avoid. But he also had seemed to understand the spirit of the man did not mean us any harm.

"You're sure?" I asked Jordan, and he gave a slight nod. I moved away, and as soon as I did the spirit collided with him, sending him back against the wall with a slam.

"Jordan, are you okay?"

His eyes flickered open, and he looked around the room as though seeing it for the first time before his eyes met mine. "You're the one who can call spirits," he said to me, but it wasn't Jordan's voice.

"I can't call them only if they're in the same vicinity. It's not a spell that pulls them to me."

"I tried to ask you to help me before, but you ignored me. I need to tell you, what happened to me was not an accident." His voice was frantic. He spoke quickly, and his voice faltered as his powers started to wane.

"Tell me now while you have time."

"Someone called me, a voice from the past. They told me they had information about my family, and it was here in Sacramento. The next day someone left a business card for a psychic on the windshield of my truck. I left right then and drove straight through to get here."

"Did you live here before?"

"No." Jordan's features wavered as the ghost fought to stay inside him and keep control of the living body he did not know how to manipulate. "Call the psychic, she has answers. I was on the phone with her when I got in the accident."

Something definitely wasn't right. It went way beyond a pushy ghost, and the fact he had nothing on him that told us much about who he was. Jordan's face crumbled in pain, but he fought against it and tried to give the spirit what it needed.

"You don't have much more time, if there's more you need to say then now is the time." I wasn't sure why some spirits were more confused than others. Some seemed perfectly coherent of what had happened to them, while many more were confused, and unaware of anything. I wondered once again if a spirit getting knocked out of a body somehow short-circuited the memory.

As the thought crossed my mind, the spirit was flung out of his body, just as Jordan collapsed. I caught him and eased him into his chair while the spirit faded away, spent from using too much energy to possess Jordan. "You're okay now. Just take it easy." I patted his chest, and his hand came up and covered mine. Warm, his hand was warm and comforting.

"I think I'm okay now," Jordan murmured.

"Come on, let's get you in the back so you can rest. I don't want to explain to anyone that you're exhausted from having a ghost possess you." He mumbled as I hefted him up and slipped his arm around my shoulder. "Come on Buddy, let's get him into the other room." No use pretending anymore. Jordan knew I could see ghosts, and he'd mentioned Buddy earlier.

We made it into the exam room, and I helped him to another room where there were no bodies and eased him onto an exam table. "Bran?"

"I'm right here, let me get you some water." I patted his hand before I hurried off to the small refrigerator where I kept an assortment of drinks. After taking a sip, he looked better, but not by much, and so far, the ghost wasn't showing itself either. Buddy stayed close to Jordan, and I wondered how I hadn't noticed that before.

"I'm okay, it just took a lot out of me. He's very strong, and very determined. I know the psychic he mentioned.

Janis. She's very popular with the paranormal world in Sacramento."

I hadn't heard of her, but I wasn't exactly proud of my ability, and kept it hidden from everyone. "How do you know her?" I finally asked as he took another sip of water.

"I went to her a few times for help with crystals. She's very good at sensing what protections you need, no matter what it's from. Plus, her brother is part of one of the best ghost hunting groups in the area. You've probably heard of them, Running Scared Paranormal Research."

"No, I don't think so. I try to stay as far away from paranormal groups as possible."

"Is that why you work at the morgue? You can see ghosts. I wouldn't think you'd want to work so close to them."

"I've asked myself that question many times. But the truth is I'd rather work with the dead than the living. It's less complicated."

"If you say so. All I know is once they know they can possess me they never stop trying. And I can't see them, but I can feel them, and all of their pain. They have a lot of pain."

"What do you mean?" He'd never mentioned any of this to me before, but now that we were both confessing, I wanted to know more.

"They sense I can feel them and most of them are desperate to either be seen or heard. But feeling is something they crave. Without their physical body the only time they feel anything is when the living passes through them," Jordan rambled.

"So, you've done this a few times." The realization hit me. He knew way more about this than I did.

"Yeah, but mostly not by choice."

Four

Jordan

He stared at me, and I knew he'd figured it out. He knew that spirits had used me before, and many times it had not ended well. "Janis can help," I croaked out, still weak from being taken over.

He turned his back to me and looked down at the floor. He wore his pain on the outside like an itchy wool blanket he couldn't discard. No one else could see it, but it weighed him down with so much grief and sadness. "All the sadness of the dead," I whispered.

"What?" he asked.

"The way you feel, it's from the dead. I was the same, but Janis showed me how to funnel that pain into a crystal. Now I know how it sounds but—"

"Jordan, if you can help me in any way at all I could use it. I've been alone in this for so long, and it's only gotten worse. When I was a kid I'd see shadows, but as I grew the spirits showed themselves to me more and more. Until finally they didn't try to hide anymore, they started trying to communicate, and once they knew I could see them and hear them, more and more of them came."

"Why would you take a job at the morgue? I mean even the hospital is questionable. There's so much death and sorrow here. And if you can see them and hear them it has to be horrible."

"No one here questions if I act strange, they all think I'm a little off anyway, so it doesn't matter. There are a lot of spirits here, but by being around them constantly it's helped me get stronger and ignore them. Most of them are only here temporarily, but there're a few that never leave."

"Bran, is there a spirit in the room now?" He looked around the room, and then down where I knew his dog was.

"Yeah, there's three. But they don't know I can see them yet," he whispered. "The guy from the accident is back, but he's confused again. Something is definitely wrong; he should have gone by now. There's an old woman I saw in the hall earlier, I think she's the one you took to the back."

"Who's the third?"

"You don't want to know."

"What do you do to block them out?" It was so odd to me that he was obviously distressed by the things he could see and hear, but he didn't seem to have any protection.

"Mostly I ignore them, but there's a lot you don't know about my past. I didn't grow up in a traditional home, which is probably why strange things don't really shock me. But that being said it would be nice to know how to protect myself."

"I'll call Janis—" My phone interrupted me, and Bran waved me off to answer it. "Hello?"

"Jordan, this is Janis. I know we haven't spoken for a time, but I think you need me. Your friend really needs me. So, as soon as you can I'd like you to meet me at my house. Your friend will need to be cleansed before he can enter, I won't risk having one of the spirits that are attracted to him brought into my home, that includes his dog."

"Uh, okay. I'll tell him. It's nearly time for lunch, I'll ask him if we can go now." I raised my brows to him while clutching the phone to my ear. He nodded his head, and I was about to tell Janis when she spoke.

"I'll see you soon, please don't take too long."

"Did you tell her we wanted to see her?" Bran asked.

"No, it's kinda weird she has a sense of things, and she doesn't doubt her ability. She acts on it." I had no idea what had made me open up to Bran. Normally I kept my ability to myself, but I was drawn to him. He was cute, but it was more than that. The power and force that emanated from him drew me in, but I wasn't sure why. Hopefully Janis would have some answers.

"Let's finish with the car accident victim, then we can go talk to your friend. I don't want to leave him the way he is now." He spoke like the man in the accident knew exactly how Bran was treating him, and I guess if anyone would know, he would.

I nodded, but normally I waited out in the outer office, and I liked it that way. I had no desire to see what he did when he performed an autopsy. "I'll just be out front. Yell if you need any help." I turned to walk away and was hit with a cold so deep it stopped me in my tracks. Then the feeling of sadness and fear hit me. I'd held it back as long as I could but now it poured down on me like a waterfall of emotions.

I hurried out to my desk and with shaking hands, I took the crystal out of the drawer again and siphoned off the feelings my body could no longer contain, and I wondered why it seemed easier when I was near Bran. But I didn't understand how his proximity could help me with an ability I'd struggled with since I was nine. That year my life changed, and no matter how good I got at dealing with it I knew I'd never have the life I had before.

My mind went back to that summer day when I was just a kid and didn't want to bother anyone about going swimming in the river behind our house. My parents had told me many times never to go there alone, and only to go in the water when one of them was with me. But I wasn't known as a kid that followed directions very well.

The last thing I remembered was how fast the water pulled me along until I hit the branch of a tree that was above the surface but was snagged underneath in the swirling depths. I woke up three days later with my parents in a hospital room, and a feeling of sorrow and dread. Somehow, I knew it was coming from my parents, and immediately on seeing my eyes open those feelings turned to joy and happiness. I didn't understand it at the time, but now I understood it far too well, and tried to avoid some emotions all together, while others I practiced blocking. My family may have been predisposed to being empaths, but none of them had to nearly die to inherit the trait. I'd always wondered if being so close to death had made me even more in tune with the feelings of the dead.

"Jordan, we've got another one," one of the nurses said, as she pushed a gurney through the doors and directly in front of my desk. "She's been hanging on for a few weeks now. But hopefully she's finally at peace." She set the clipboard with the patient's information on my desk, and without another word walked away. None of them stayed long. I hadn't been here long, and I learned very quickly how the rest of the hospital staff avoided this area.

Bombarded with emotions from confusion to fear, I clenched my eyes shut and forced myself to take a deep breath. Asking myself once again why I thought this job was a good idea. I forced myself to pick up the clipboard and after setting it on the top of the body I wheeled it toward the door to the back. "Come on Edith, time to meet Bran," I whispered.

Five

Bran

I had so many questions for Jordan, but most of them I was afraid to ask. I'd grown up with this power, and through it all my family had encouraged me to use it, to grow it and nurture it. But now I wanted it gone. I hoped to be able to help people, but there was no helping the dead.

"Doctor, can you hear me?" The accident victim was back. He didn't look as fully formed as he had earlier, but now he knew for a fact I could see him.

"Yes, I can hear you. Can you tell me what you were doing here?" I tried again to get more information, but he looked away and ignored me.

"My family will be disappointed in me, but I suppose there's nothing that can be done now. When you meet with Janis tell her I said to tell you everything. She'll understand."

"Is there someone you want us to notify? There wasn't anything on you that told us who we should call."

"My family was done with me years ago. The person that posted online is a good friend. My only friend, and I'd appreciate you letting them know what happened, so they don't keep looking for me."

Just then the door swung open, and Jordan walked in pushing a gurney. The old woman from earlier walked right behind him. "Sorry, we had another one come in. I'll just push it into the back."

"Thanks Jordan," I mumbled, and the old woman once again rushed up to get in my face.

"You can try to ignore me all you want. But if you won't give me a moment of your time I will make you miserable the time that I'm here," she threatened just as Jordan walked back through the room.

"Are you nearly done?" he asked.

"Yes, I can leave it where I'm at now, let me just move him to the cooler then we can go meet with your friend." It wasn't that I was anxious to meet with her, I was actually dreading it. But I needed a break from the barrage of demands from the spirit world for just a few hours.

"Okay, I'll let them know out front," Jordan said as he walked out the door to his desk.

I covered the man up again and pushed him back to the cold room with both him and the old lady right behind me. I didn't acknowledge either of them as I walked out to Jordan. "Are you ready?"

"Yes," he said as he took his phone and shoved it in his pocket and slipped on a jacket.

We walked out into the hall and past the front desk, only pausing a moment to tell the person in charge we'd be back after lunch. With a nod from them we were on our way. Both of us took a deep breath after stepping outside, and it wasn't hard to see Jordan's shoulders finally relax after we were in the parking garage. "I'll drive." I said and pressed my key fob making the lights flash.

"Is this better?" I asked after both of us were inside.

"Yeah, I mean I can still feel your emotions, but it's not as intense as the ones inside the hospital," Jordan said, and buckled his belt.

"Can I ask you something?"

"Sure," he said and turned to face me.

"Why did you take a job where you'd not only be exposed to death, but also to fear and desperation. It seems like the worst job an empath could ever ask for."

"Yeah, it hasn't been fun. But it has helped me learn how to block out a lot of those emotions. And the crystals Janis gave me have helped a lot too."

"The crystals really have helped?" I was so curious about this woman who he said was such a strong psychic, and wondered if my mother would know her.

"Yes, that's what Janis does. When we get there, she'll read you and tell you what you need. Sometimes it doesn't make sense, and other times it's perfectly clear. But either way, she's rarely wrong."

Very few people knew anything about my past, let alone everything. I worried how Jordan would react once he knew, if in fact she could read me as easily as he seemed to think she could. My mother had tried many spells to not only bind my powers to other people, but to help me control them. Because before I started working at the morgue, I had no control over the spirits who chose to approach me. If nothing else, being exposed to them all day had made me stronger, and less shocked by what I saw, and what they said.

Jordan showed me the way to her house, and I was happy to see it wasn't far. We pulled up to a very average looking house along a tree-lined street in one of the older areas of Sacramento. As soon as I turned the engine off the door swung open.

"Come on, she's waiting," Jordan said, and without another word got out of the car.

"Jordan, I hope you're doing your daily crystal therapy. I worry about you getting too overwhelmed with the emotions of the dead and living now that you're working at the hospital." She pulled him in for a hug and looked past him to me.

"Bran, welcome." She held Jordan at arms-length and smiled at him before turning and walking back inside her house. "Gentlemen, we don't have much time. I wanted to cleanse you before you entered, but I don't sense any spirits with you besides your familiar.

"Oh, I don't have a fam—we can talk later," I said and watched her walk inside.

Jordan gave me a tightlipped grin before following her. . I hesitated a moment before gathering myself and following them to the kitchen where they were both seated at the table. She had a tarot deck on the table in front of her and multiple protections in place.

"I know you recognize most of what you see. I also know you haven't been completely honest with Jordan. Now is the time, everything must be told. Jordan you also need to clarify your power, so Bran knows what he's dealing with. Jordan, you begin," Janis said without even an introduction or explanation.

Jordan took a deep breath and began. "When I was nine years old, I died."

SIX

Jordan

"I went to the river behind my house by myself and I don't remember how, but I ended up in the water. They didn't find me until I'd been under for a while, but they were able to resuscitate me and brought me back. When I woke up, the first thing I was aware of was the emotions that seemed to be flooding the room. At that time, I didn't understand what it was, and I thought I was going insane. But my parents explained to me that most of my relatives had the same ability in an array of strengths. But none of them had gotten it after a traumatic event.

Anytime I was near someone I could tell exactly how they were feeling. Then it started expanding to the dead. I went to a funeral for an elderly relative when I was thirteen, and walking through the cemetery was like walking through different areas of emotion. Again, I didn't understand what it was, but now I do. And Janis has helped me to learn my limits, and ways to relieve the pain that goes along with feeling their emotions."

"Can I ask you something?" Bran asked.

I nodded and waited while Janis lit some sage and proceeded to wave it around him. "Sorry, but your connection with the dead is very strong. I won't risk them staying here after you leave."

Bran ignored the smoke and looked at me again. "Why would you work at the morgue if it's so painful for you to be exposed to so many emotions. It has to be the worst place you could ever work."

"I'll explain that to you Bran, but first. Please explain to Jordan how your skill works." Janis folded her hands on the table after saging me and looked at me with eyes full of expectation and curiosity.

"My mother was a necromancer. She was part of a coven, and her specialty was calling on the dead for any information they may need. Her power grew, and soon she started to use that power in ways to make money for herself or to help our family. The coven didn't like this and forbade her from using her power. For more than a year she didn't call upon the dead, and during that time she got pregnant with me.

From the day I was born, I could see and hear spirits. But I learned as a young boy to ignore them. For a while they left me alone, but I could feel on the edge of my senses. Just far enough away to give me space, but close enough to let me know they were there, like shadows. When I turned thirteen everything changed. We moved to a different house, and as soon as we walked in, I could sense there was a spirit there.

That night an old woman crawled up on my bed. 'I know you can see me,' she screamed in my face. I waited for my parents to come into my room, but they didn't, and the next day neither of them mentioned hearing an old woman screaming. At that very moment, I knew I was on my own and I needed to find a way to deal with the spirits or they'd drive me insane."

"Your mom wasn't aware of the old lady?" I asked because if his mom could also sense spirits I couldn't understand why she'd leave her son unprotected.

"She later admitted to me that she knew, but she wanted to see how I handled it. It was a test."

"She had to know you'd be terrified."

"Yes, she was counting on that. She hoped to show me how strong my powers could be without any magic or spells. But all she did was show me how much I did not want to be in that world. Her coven had thrown her out after she had no power, and I knew they'd do the same to me in a heartbeat."

"You were wise not to put your trust in them. Not all covens would abandon a member, but sadly the one your parents were in was not only using white magic," Janis said. "Now I have to ask you both something. Have you noticed when you two are together there is a quieting that happens in your mind?"

Bran and I looked at each other and I knew he was going over the days events the same way I was. When we were both together the spirits seemed to back off and not be quite so aggressive, even though I couldn't hear them, it seemed more relaxed when he was in the room with me.

"I'm not sure," I said. "Bran has a spirit dog that's always with him, I think he helps me a lot. He seems to sense when I need his contact."

"His name is Buddy, and he was my dog when I was a kid. When I was afraid of what spirits might approach me, he always protected me. He could sense them when he was alive, and after his death he still protects me."

"He chose to stay with you rather than move on. He knew you needed him and chose to become a familiar and protector to you," Janis said.

"When the spirit of the guy showed up today, Buddy wasn't worried. He leaned on me, but he didn't see him as a threat."

"Do you know this man's name?" Janis asked.

"Justice Rafferty. I tried to find out more about him, but I didn't have much luck other than a post on social media that said his friends were looking for him."

"He said that you would know more about him, and that he'd contacted you" Bran handed her the card he'd found in Justice's wallet and watched Janis who never reacted at all.

She turned the card over in her hand but didn't read it. "I heard from him about a week ago. He'd gotten involved with the wrong people and was trying to find a way to get away from them."

"What do you mean the wrong people?" I asked.

"Justice had the same ability you do Bran. His parents deserted him years ago when he was just a child. They thought he was possessed by demons and couldn't wait to get away from him. He was on his way to me to learn how to protect himself from the spirits that had harassed him his whole life. Where you have learned to protect yourself, he had no such protections. He thought he was insane."

"I wish I'd known. I'm not sure I could have helped him, but I could be there to offer support."

"Has he reached out to you?" Janis asked.

"When I first saw his spirit, he was very confused like most of the newly dead are. He knew I could see him, and he kept trying to get me to notice him. But then he entered Jordan, and it got even more confusing."

"What exactly do you mean by that?" She narrowed her eyes and looked at Bran with a scrutinizing stare before turning it on me.

"I allowed him to take over my body. I know you warned me against it, but we couldn't find any information about him, and he was so confused and filled with pain," Jordan said and avoided looking directly at Janis.

"How was your pain when you did this?" she asked.

"All pain left me, but I'd just siphoned off what was there before I tried this. So, I'm not sure if it was because I had already drawn the pain out, or if letting him into my body helped."

"Then I guess we'll need to see what happens. Ready to let another spirit in?" Janis asked and rolled up her sleeves.

seven

Bran

"You just happen to have a spirit hanging around that will be willing to possess me?" Jordan asked, but Janis's eyes were on me.

"Is there a spirit near?" she asked.

My eyes fluttered shut, I hated to open up my senses because yes, there was always a spirit nearby. Right now, out front of her house there was a man who had died while jogging, and in the back yard there was another but I wasn't sure who or what it was. "Yes, there's two outside, one in the front by the street, and one out back."

"Let's go out back. My neighbors don't need to see any more than they have to." Janis chose a few items: crystals, herbs, and things I didn't know about and had never seen before.

Jordan and I stood, and he hesitated a moment before we both followed Janis to her backyard. She set up the items she'd brought on the patio table, and took a seat at one of the chairs directing us to do the same.

"Give me just a moment, I want to make sure that this spirit is contained and cannot enter my house or either of us," she said to Jordan. "Have you had spirits take over your body before?"

"Yes, a few times. But it wasn't my choice. This time was different. Something told me that's what I needed to do to help."

"You're a good man Jordan. But I should warn you, inviting a spirit in is never advisable. Some will leave without a problem, while others will not. Then we get into an exorcism, and well I'm not really equipped to do that, nor do I want to." She spoke as though she was talking about having a friend come over that you no longer wanted around rather than a ghost entering a living person's body. And somehow, I found it both horrifying, and strangely comforting.

"I know," Jordan said. "I took your advice and started reading up on spirits, and there's so much out there. Most of it is crap, I'm sure. But I have a little more information to fall back on than I did before."

"You said you'd been using crystals to draw off the pain?"

"Yes. It helps, just like you said it would. Maybe clearing my aura helped me have more control."

A serene smile spread on Janis's lips, and she glanced at Jordan. "You've learned a lot in a short amount of time."

"I'm tired of fighting it and being in pain from the battle. If I can help them, I will."

"Very well. Bran, can you please make contact with the spirit?"

My eyes widened; I was listening so intently that I was shocked when the conversation turned to me. "Yes. It's a child and he seems to stay over at the base of the big tree." I walked to the area of the yard in the back corner and watched as the child peeked around the trunk of the massive tree. "It's okay, I won't hurt you. Would it be okay if you met my friends?"

"I'm all alone here," he said in a small voice.

"I know, but my friends and I might be able to help you cross over. Would you like that?" I wasn't sure I knew how to do that, but I wanted to give him some hope. Janis nodded when I looked her way, and Jordan walked over closer to me.

The ghost popped out of view, and reappeared again on a branch high above us, and didn't say a word. Instead, he stared at Jordan as he walked up to my side. "My friend can't hear or see you like I can, but he can sense you." The ghost looked between the two of us before disappearing again and appearing in front of Jordan. He was dressed in turn of the century garb, with a white shirt, suspenders and dark pants that were too short for him. Scruffy blonde hair and a dirty face told of hard days, and who knew what other perils.

Jordan nodded and the child ghost ran toward him. A burst of wind hit him, blowing his hair back as he braced for the impact he seemed to sense. When his eyes met mine again, I knew it wasn't Jordan.

"I want to go home. I've been looking for my mom and dad, but I can't find them." His voice took on the quality of a child, and even though my logical mind told me Jordan was standing in front of me, my senses told me this wasn't him anymore. One look in his eyes and I knew for sure, it wasn't him. It was different than it had been with the accident victim earlier. This was a ghost who had been here for years, and understood he was stuck.

"We can help you little one," Janis said, as she slowly walked closer to him. "If you want to go to the other side we can help. Is that what you want?"

"Yes ma'am, I want to see my mom again." His lip quivered, and seeing Jordan show so much emotion had me choking down the lump in my throat.

"Okay little one come here." She held her hands out to him and he took them, for just a moment the shimmer of them not being completely in sync shown on Jordan's hands. But Janis smiled as though this was something she did all the time and there was nothing to fear.

She started to chant, and I was taken back to the years my mother did the same thing, only her chanting was for her own enrichment, not to help another. Magic, or something like it swirled around us all, and the hair on my arms and the back of my neck stood up. Jordan's eyes were locked on Janis, and a peaceful smile shone on his lips.

"Go now child, when you see the light that is your chance to go to your family. They're waiting for you there and can't wait to see you."

He turned and I would have sworn his face was illuminated and for just a moment it wasn't Jordan standing there, it was the small ghost I'd seen earlier. But now he was happy, and eager to go. He walked into a bright light and disappeared. Jordan was left standing there a moment, a bright smile on his face, and a tear slowly trailing down his cheek.

I rushed at him and pulled him into my arms. "Are you okay?"

"Yeah, it's just—a lot" He breathed out and I felt his body relax against mine.

"You did it, you helped him cross over. I never believed it could really happen."

"The things your mother did to spirits were very harmful to the natural balance of the spirit realm and our own. But there's something special about the two of you. You're very much like two sides of the same coin, but together your powers seem more contained, and more focused. Jordan did you have any pain when you came into contact with the spirit?" I released him from my arms but kept him close as he spoke to Janis. I wasn't ready for him to be too far away just yet, and no way was I going to try to question why that was.

EIGHT

Jordan

Janis was happy with what she'd seen, it was obvious by her expression. But Bran was concerned. I didn't understand all that had happened to him, but I didn't want him to feel alone in this anymore. We both had similar yet different abilities, but Janis was right. Together our powers were more contained, more focused.

"What did you mean about what my mother did?" Bran asked.

"Something has upset the natural order. I'm sorry but I wasn't completely honest with you earlier. The spirit you came into contact with at the morgue was not meant to die. He'd been consulting me for a while now. Some time ago he had a meeting with another psychic, and after taking a lot of his money, she didn't like it when that money was going to dry up. So instead of leaving well enough alone, she cursed him. But not a curse of bad luck or something like that. No, she cursed him to be trapped here wandering for all of eternity."

"Who could have that power?" Bran asked.

"Not many are capable of such a thing, but a strong Necromancer could accomplish it with some help," Janis said. She lit a bundle of sage and waved the smoke around her yard. "Although why would someone want to curse someone in such a way?"

"Maybe they needed to use a spirit for some reason, and wanted to make sure it was obedient." Somehow, I knew it was true as soon as the words were out of my mouth. "Can you tell us why Justice Rafferty had contacted you?" I asked.

Janis tapped her lip with her finger as she continued to walk around her yard. "I don't normally like to disclose those things. People come to me for help, and by the time they do, the last thing they want is for it to be spread all over the news. But this case is different." She walked over to the table where she'd set her tarot deck and sat down.

"Justice came to me out of fear. He'd been having dreams telling of someone gathering an army of spirits. He wasn't sure how it would happen, or who would cause it.

But he knew he'd be involved. I don't think he suspected he'd end up as one of the foot soldiers in this strange war."

"Is that what you really think it is?" All of this was weird. But a war of ghosts?

"My brother and his friends are part of a paranormal research team. Lately there's more activity, and even more that isn't reported that I can feel. He knows it too, he's connected to a part of the other side in ways we're just beginning to understand. But we both sense something has changed. And according to my readings you two are meant to be a bridge between the two worlds."

"What do you mean?" Bran asked. "I've spent years learning to ignore the ghosts that constantly try to get my attention."

"Have you asked them what they want?" Janis asked as easily if she were talking about an annoying neighbor.

"No!" Bran nearly shouted. "I don't think you understand how aggressive they are, and how far they'll go to get the living to notice them."

"I know exactly how far they'll go. Why do you think my home is warded against them? I knew that my herbs and crystals were not enough to protect me if they truly wanted to get to me. And if the signs and my cards are right, they are going to be looking for people like me."

"What do you mean?"

"I think anyone who they perceive as a threat will end up like Justice. Trapped here and confused without a way to end his suffering."

"Who would do this?" I asked. None of this made sense. "What would they hope to accomplish by using spirits to do their bidding." Janis watched as my mind raced. Then finally Jordan placed his hand on top of mine.

"If they can control spirits they can unleash a power on mankind that we'd have no way of defending. If they can enslave a ghost and force them to do what they want they could have whatever they want," Jordan said, his eyes wide with the realization of just how bad this could be.

"There has to be a way to stop this from happening," I said, and looked between the two of them.

"I'm not so sure about that. We don't know for certain who has set these actions in motion and until they decide to reveal themselves, we very well may never know. But we can make sure that we're ready for them," Janis said. "I want to speak to Justice, and see if we can help him cross over the same way we did for the child. If it works, we may just have a chance at slowing them down or stopping them."

"But what's to stop whoever it is from creating more? Or what if they already have?" I wanted to believe her, but I had serious doubts that the three of us could protect anyone.

"The paranormal community in Sacramento has grown lately. There's a group of urban explorers who have a member I've been working with. It seems she was taken to a remote cabin and was endowed with the ability to speak to not only spirits but demons. We've all tried to figure out what happened to her, but I think in some way what happened to her may be related to what happened to Justice."

"So she's like Jordan?" Bran asked.

"No, her ability has to do with ancient symbols that are on her skin but can only be seen when she's in the vicinity of a demon or spirit. She can't control her interactions, and while she can sense both, she was not born into this life. Her powers are from her markings."

"Where did she get the markings?" Bran whispered.

Janis was deep in thought for a moment before she looked up at the two of us. "I'm not sure, but I feel there is a link between her power and Justice's spirit being ripped from him and tethered here."

"Do we need her to help?" I asked.

"No, not yet. For now we're going to help Justice move on, then we're going to spread protection around the city.

We may not be able to save everyone, but we can make it harder for whoever it is to take more souls."

"What if they figure out it's us?" Bran asked.

"I'm counting on it. Then we'll know who we're up against and we can get ready for what comes next. All we can do now is weaken them while we gather anyone who can help and make it harder for them to make more spirits."

"I want to help Justice if I can. He needs to move on to find peace," I said, and was met with a smile from Janis.

"If you're ready, I think we should go to the morgue. We'll need to do this as soon as we can so he's not trapped here." Janis grabbed a few supplies and promptly stuffed them into a tote bag before slipping on her jacket. "I'm ready to go if you are."

Bran's eyes met mine and his nod of determination was all it took to get me going. "Let's go. I want to end his suffering as soon as I can." The three of us walked outside and Buddy was next to us as we went to the car.

"You're a good boy Buddy," Janis said as she slid into her seat and patted the seat next to her for him. Even though she couldn't see him, it was obvious she knew he was there and knowing he trusted her made me trust her even more than I already did.

NINE

Bran

The three of us walked into the hospital like it was any other day, and we weren't going there with a task that was important to every person here. Janis clutched a crystal in her hand and kept her head down all the way to the morgue.

"I thought you couldn't see them?" Jordan asked.

"Oh, I can't but their energy is so strong here it's like a million voices screaming my name all at once."

We hurried to the back room, and Buddy stayed close to Janis, and I thought I noticed her reach for him. "Thank you, Buddy," she murmured.

The ghost of the old woman was still wandering around blindly, while Justice was nowhere in sight. "Do you see him?" Janis asked.

"No, not yet." It was odd, he'd been here when we'd left. Even though he was weak he was still communicating.

"I'm here," Justice said, as he glided across the room. He glanced at Janis and then back at me. "Are you going to help me?"

"Janis is going to try."

"Justice, I'm sorry for what happened. I'm not sure we know everything that has happened or what will happen. But I have a bad feeling about what's coming, and I think there are forces trying to bind spirits to this side of the realm for their own uses," Janis said.

"Do you know why?" he asked.

"No, but we're going to do all we can to find out and stop them from whatever plan they have. I think the first thing we need to do is try to help you to cross over. Since your death seems somehow connected I worry there's a reason you're still here, and I'm sorry to say, I don't think it's good."

"Janis, I know we only spoke a few times, but I trust you. I don't want to hurt anyone, but I also don't understand what's happened to me. I want peace. If you can help me find that, I'd be grateful." His voice warbled, and his form shimmered as he spoke, and I wondered if he was getting weaker the longer he was here.

"Bran and Jordan together can help you, together their power will guide you," Janis explained. "I'll just be a few moments while I get everything ready. She looked around the room before setting her bag down on a counter and going through the same routine she'd done earlier at her house. First, she lit a bundle of sage and other herbs and started to clear the room.

But this time, things did not go as smoothly as they had earlier. As she walked around the room spreading the scented smoke throughout, the temperature in the room dropped, and a mist formed along the floor. Janis ignored this and cleansed every part of the room.

The old woman from earlier pounded on the door and asked to be let in. But Janis either couldn't hear her or ignored her and set out everything she had earlier. "Okay I want us to do exactly what we did earlier. Justice you'll need to enter Jordan's body again."

Jordan looked nervous, and instinctively I reached for his hand. "It'll be okay. I'll make sure you're safe, and Justice is guided to the other side."

Jordan nodded and stepped closer to where Justice's spirit waited. "Everything is ready," Janis said, and started chanting.

Justice floated closer to Jordan who nodded at him. "Go ahead, and don't worry, we're going to help your pain."

Justice moved closer to him and entered Jordan's body. Just like before he appeared as a shimmer on Jordan's skin. As Janis chanted, something changed. Jordan's arms started to glow, and he clutched his head in pain. "Something's wrong," he yelled.

"Jordan!" I rushed toward him, but something stopped me, a force that seemed to encircle him. Janis looked up at us her eyes wide with fright. She was focused on Jordan, and I turned again to him and noticed the glow had changed, and symbols started to appear.

Janis ran to the wall and drew out a series of symbols with a piece of charcoal, and while I didn't know exactly what it was for, I knew what it was. She cut her hand and slapped it on the symbol, and at the same time Justice's spirit was thrown from Jordan.

"What was that?" Jordan gasped.

"This is bad boys. This is very very bad," Janis said, and started to gather up the things she'd brought.

"What were those symbols, I don't understand why would my arms start to take them on?" Jordan's voice grew more frantic as Janis started to walk to the door.

"There's more here than I can help with. This is not a spirit we're dealing with although it wants you to believe that." She glanced around the room, and a low rumbling growl sounded, that seemed to come from everywhere and nowhere.

The two of us followed her out the door and I ignored the old woman and was relieved to see Buddy sitting next to Jordan's desk. "What happened in there?" I asked Janis.

"This is not a spirit. Whatever is in there is from the demon realm. The only thing I can imagine is that Justice was possessed before he died. He may not have even known, but those symbols on his arms keep his spirit tied to the demon or whatever it is."

"Are we safe here?" Jordan asked, his face pale and a bead of sweat running down his brow.

Janis stopped then and turned to face us both. "No. There's nothing more we can do. I need to see what I can find out, and when I do, I'll contact you. But until then, stay safe. All that's left now is to save who we can."

"What do you mean?" I asked.

"The battle has begun."

EPILOGUE

Jordan

It had been three months since we'd tried to help Justice move to the light, and three months since everything had changed. "Where do you think his spirit went?" I asked Bran for the umpteenth time.

"I'm not sure. Maybe it didn't go anywhere." Bran was reading a chart while Buddy sat on the floor by his feet watching. Buddy was always on alert now and didn't allow other spirits to approach either of us. At first, we thought he was just being cautious, but then we noticed there were many more spirits wandering around than there had been and most were even more aggressive to get us to notice them.

"Maybe. I should probably call Janis again," I said.

"Have you heard anything?" Bran asked looking up from his work.

"No, the last time I talked to her she said she was still doing research." It was odd. I hadn't known Janis long, but this didn't seem normal, and it felt like there was way more happening than any of us were aware of. I looked at the symbol she'd drawn on the wall that was still there, complete with the handprint in her own blood.

"Maybe we should start learning what some of these symbols mean?" Bran stepped closer to the charcoal drawing, and reached his hand toward it. Just before he touched it his arm started to glow and the shape of one of the symbols that had been on the spirits arms started to appear on his. "What the fuck?" He scrubbed at his arms and tried to brush it off, and eventually the symbol faded.

"We need to go talk to Janis, I'm tired of waiting to see what happens next."

"Yeah, its unnerving. I don't understand why the symbol needs to be here, and why we need more protection now than we needed before," I said. "Let me message Janis and see if she's avail—" The alert of an incoming message stopped me, and I checked to see it was from Janis saying we should go to her house as soon as possible.

"We can go now," Bran said, "I'm tired of waiting." He hurried to put away the body he'd been working on, and the two of us rushed to the parking garage and decided I'd drive there. Jordan waited for Buddy to get in the back, which was funny since he was a spirit and could just appear there if he wanted, but Jordan was so used to him being there he had a hard time ignoring him.

"What do you think is going on?" I asked as we made the short drive.

"Well, I don't think she would have messaged us if she didn't know something. I mean we've heard nothing for months." He was annoyed, which I understood.

"I guess we'll know soon enough." I turned onto her street and was surprised to see so many cars. We found a space a few doors down and hurried to her house.

"Jordan and Bran, thank you so much for coming on such short notice. But I knew you'd want to be here," Janis said as she held the door open for us. "I've brought everyone together who I think can help us. There's quite a few, but I promise we are all connected." I wasn't sure what she meant by that, but we followed her through her house to the backyard.

There was a group of people speaking to each other in her backyard, some I recognized and others I didn't. "I told you about my brother James, well this is his group of paranormal investigators." She introduced us all, and they looked at us with the same confused look I'm sure we wore.

"Janis what's this all about?" her brother asked.

"James, something is happening, and we're all going to have to work together if we want to have a chance at stopping it. Some events have already been put in motion that I cannot control beyond slowing them down."

A woman walked closer to us and rolled her sleeves up as she walked. "You don't know me, but after talking with Janis, I think in some ways we're connected. I'm Sophia, and I'm the one Janis told you about who was found alone in the woods. Since then, I have these marks that glow when I'm near a demon or spirit."

"Only when you're near one? Sort of like a warning?" I asked.

"Sort of. A while back Dane was marked the same way. Both of us have noticed some changes the past three months."

"What kind of changes?" Bran asked.

"Normally our marks are invisible, or in some cases they appear like a tattoo, but they fade eventually. Now they look like this." She completely rolled up her sleeves revealing mark after mark, all outlined in deep black lines and glowing. A man accompanied by another man who looked like he'd tear apart anyone who touched the first guy, walked over and showed us his neck and arms that looked the same.

"I'm Dane. I got these marks after I was possessed, but now there're so many spirits it feels like we're constantly fighting to keep them out."

"Mind if I?" Bran asked and took first Sophia, and then Dane's arm in his hands. "What do you mean there're so many?"

"Haven't you noticed how many are trapped here now?" One of the men that Janis had said worked with her brother asked.

Obviously tired of pretending Bran answered. "I've noticed. And they're more aggressive."

"If we don't do something now they'll outnumber the living, and if the right person is pulling the strings they'll be able to overcome the boundaries that prevent them from taking over whatever body they want. If that happens, we'll have no hope of the living having control ever again," Janis said. "All of us will need to work together using your unique abilities if this is going to work. Right now they're preparing to take control by using a mark borne of black magic and mysticism that has never been used, and could prove catastrophic if it works or if it fails. I can see the outcome both ways, and neither are good. I can also see the person working on it, but I cannot pinpoint where they are."

"Why is that?" Jordan asked.

"They're using a spell to block me and any other psychic that might try to stop them."

"So, they know we're coming?" Janis's brother asked.

"Yes James, they know, but if we don't try to stop them, and stop them now, then everything is lost."

"What do you mean everything?" James asked, and another man leaned against him.

"The world we know will cease to exist. Everything will be taken by the dead."

A shocked murmur rolled through the group, but eventually a few came forward and spoke to Janis. "What's next? We're not going down without a fight."

"Jason, I knew you would be willing to fight," Janis said with a smile.

"We'll all fight," a few more said and everyone joined in a group near the house.

"I hoped you all felt this way. Some of you may know this enemy, as you've fought them before. I'm afraid I do know who it is, but I was hesitant to tell you."

"Who is it?" Jason asked.

Janis tapped her lip before looking at each of us. "I'm afraid the wraith has returned. And he's not alone this time, a human has joined with him in a bid to gain power and control."

A rumble of voices all talked after she'd said this, and even though Bran and I didn't know exactly what the wraith was, it was easy to see most of the people in the group did, and they were not happy to hear this was who was involved.

"How are the marks connected? None of that happened when we dealt with it before," another man asked.

"The same person who marked Sophia is the one who works with the wraith, and I'm afraid you're not going to like hearing the rest of this Bran."

His head snapped up and he looked around the group. Instinctively I moved closer to him and put my hand on his back wanting him to know I was with him even if no one else in the group was.

"My mother," he whispered, and Janis nodded.

"It seems she did not need the power of her coven once she found black magic and the creatures who would use her. We can't do this without your help, but I understand how that would be a tough choice for you to make."

"There's no choice to make. Tell me what we need to do."

"Nothing. For now, we plan, and we build our own protections just as she's doing. But lucky for us we're not without lots of talent that she doesn't know about."

I knew Buddy was leaning on his leg when he stopped himself from reaching down to him. "Whatever you need me for I'm in. There's no way I'm willing to stand back and watch our world be destroyed."

"I hoped you'd say that" Janis said. "Now, if everyone agrees. Let's get to work."

I wasn't sure what work we'd be doing, but I knew without a doubt I was willing to do whatever I could to protect Bran. In the months I'd known him I felt more connected to him than I had with anyone ever, and I wasn't willing to have that connection severed by a necromancer intent on a power grab. Even if it was his mother I'd do what I could to protect him. And Buddy.

ABOUT THE AUTHOR

BL Maxwell grew up in a small town listening to her grandfather spin tales about his childhood. Later she became an avid reader and after a certain vampire series she became obsessed with fanfiction. She soon discovered Slash fanfiction and later discovered the MM genre and was hooked.

Many years later, she decided to take the plunge and write down some of the stories that seem to run through her head late at night when she's trying to sleep.

BL Maxwell loves to hear from readers who enjoy her stories, so feel free to reach out at any of these links:

Website: https://blmaxwellwriter.com/ (Free book)

Newsletter: https://sendfox.com/blmaxwell

Facebook: https://www.facebook.com/bl.maxwell.35/

Bookbub: https://www.bookbub.com/profile/bl-maxwell

BingeBooks: https://bingebooks.com/profile/blmaxwell

ALSO BY BL MAXWELL

Thank you for reading Just Another Day At The Morgue. This book is the bridge between The Mystical Markings books, and the Valley Ghosts Series and the beginning of their own series Spirit Boys. This is how Bran and Jordan get involved with Janis and the guys from Running Scared Paranormal Research. The Things We Lose is the first time Bran and and Jordan work with the team, but their story doesn't begin there. Preorder Spirit Boys Book One: Dead Things. Availalbe March 14, 2024 https://books2read.c om/DeadThingsSB1

Enjoy a FREE copy of The Cemetery Tour a Valley Ghosts Short Story. This gives a glimpse of the Running Scared guys finding out something has changed in the spirit world.

https://dl.bookfunnel.com/ev7b5oxqaz

It was just a fun Halloween activity until the ghosts showed up.

Jason Thomas has always loved the supernatural, and anything to do with ghosts. But when it comes to going on haunted tours he'd rather not. His boyfriend Wade books a tour for them at the local cemetery before Halloween thinking it would be fun way to get in the mood for the holiday.

Being connected to the other side of the veil, it doesn't take long for Wade to start noticing a few strange happenings. When ghosts from the past show themselves followed by other paranormal events, they both know there is more going on than a haunted cemetery tour.

This is a Valley Ghosts short story and also foretells events that happen in The Things We Lose. #MM Paranormal Romance, #FREE reads, #Ghost Story

This is a companion book, Bran and Jordan help Janis and the Running Scared guys battle evil.

The Things We Lose

Mystical Markings Book Two
https://mybook.to/TTWLose
Book One: The Things We Find: https://mybook.to/TheThingsWeFIND

Dane Jones has been touched by the spirit world. Once his powers were awakened by a cursed object, he tried to find peace with them. But the forces from beyond don't play by the rules, and soon he's wondering why he thought he had any hope of control over them.

Griff Warren loves Dane, and no matter how weird things may seem, he'll always be there for him. But strange occurrences make him question if Dane's keeping a secret, or if there's more to the strange marks Dane bears.

Dane and Griff are thrown into more supernatural trouble than they can handle, and Janis, their psychic guide, knows it. She arranges for help from The Running Scared Paranormal guys and two strangers from the morgue, Bran and Jordan. First, they'll lose their abilities, next they'll have their powers challenged, and if they can't stop what has been put into motion, no one will survive. #mmparanormalromance #supernatural #ghosthorror #urbanfantasy #gayromance

https://mybook.to/ColdBloodWarmHeart
Cold Blood Warm Heart

A Consortium Trilogy Short Story
Leon is adjusting to his new existence as a vampire, but so far Ben has kept him safely isolated in the wilderness of Alaska where he was created.

It's past time for Leon to prove he can control his urges and Ben thinks he has the perfect solution. He wants Leon to spend time with his friends Brennan and Lucas, and hopes his new mate is ready to be out in the world of humans.

Ben and Leon are newly mated vampires trying to find their place in the world. Somehow spending Christmas with two more vampires is the least shocking thing in this new world Leon is trying to navigate.
#ParanormalRomance, #MMParanormal, #FatedMates, #Vampires

Enjoy a Free copy of A Night To Remember . A short story with Andy and Link.

https://blmaxwellwriter.com/free-reads/

Faded Dreams:

https://mybook.to/FadedDreamsRTR2

Green Eyed Boy, Lobster Tales Book One

https://mybook.to/GreenEyedBoy

Brown Eyed Boy, Lobster Tales Book Two, New Release

https://mybook.to/BrownEyedBoy

BETTER TOGETHER Series

Better Together

Chains Required

The First Twelve

The Better Together Boxset

VALLEY GHOSTS Series

Ghost Hunted

Ghost Haunted

Ghost Trapped

Ghost Hexed

Ghost Handled

Ghost Shadow

Haunting Destiny

THE STONE Series

Stone Under Skin

Blood Beneath Stone

Stone Hearts

The Stone Series Box Set

SMALL TOWN CITY series

Remember When

A Night to Remember (Short Story)
Try To Forget
Try To Remember (Short Story)
One Last Chance

CONSORTIUM TRILOGY

Burning Addiction
Freezing Aversion
Cold Blood Warm Heart (Short Story)

FOUR PACKS Trilogy

The Slow Death
The Ultimate Sacrifice
The Final Salvation

BLINDING LIGHT Series

Blinding Light
Faded Dreams
Just The Right Chord (Short Story)

STANDALONE

The List

Double Black Diamonds

Ride: The Chance of a Lifetime

Check Yes or No

A Ghost of a Chance

Tutu

Salt & Lime

Amos Ridge

Six Months

Ten or Fifteen Miles

The Snake in the Castle

A Beach Far Away

The Things We Find

Blinding Light

Peppermint Mocha Kisses

Spirits, Teeth and Wings

A Taste of Paranormal Romance

BL Maxwell

https://mybook.to/SpiritsTeethWings

Try a small taste of three paranormal series featuring different creatures of the night. Ghost hunters, vampires, and gargoyles, all with their stories to tell. Each of them hoping to somehow find their other half in the strange world they live in.

Ghost Hunted:

Proving ghosts are real is something Jason Thomas had always dreamed of. Visiting the haunted places, he'd been obsessed with since he was a kid, and playing amateur ghost hunters with his best friend Wade, is a passion that's only grown. As the years passed, Jason's fascination with ghosts was too big to contain, and he'd drag Wade along to different haunted houses or hotels, always hoping to see an actual ghost.

Wade Rivers has always loved spending time with Jason, even if it meant he'd have to endure another creepy, supposedly haunted location. Before he knew it, Wade's feelings for Jason deepened from friendship into something more. Unfortunately, so did his fear of the places Jason wanted to explore.

The chance to spend a weekend alone in a famous haunted house was too much for Jason to resist, and almost too much for Wade to endure. He knew going to the deserted house was everything Jason had ever dreamed of, so Wade tried to put his fears aside. But when strange things start to happen, admitting to Jason how he feels suddenly isn't the scariest thing Wade will encounter.

A friends to lovers, paranormal romantic thriller.

Stone Under Skin:

Ankit has lived many lifetimes. Once, long ago, he was made of stone, and marked with symbols and sigils meant to safeguard him and allow him to protect and serve others. He's a living gargoyle now, cursed to live as a human; always watching, at all times aware, and constantly searching for his fated one.

While walking home from his job as a librarian, Ethan Lewis is beaten and robbed. Ankit stumbles upon him, and instantly recognizes him as the man he's fated to. He helps him back to his apartment, and after tending his injuries, watches over him.

Fate has woven their lives together for centuries, but in every lifetime, they could never live freely, or love each other as Ankit has often dreamed of. To change their destiny, they'll fight together with other gargoyles, and a young watcher, who is unaware of the tremendous power she possesses. This will be the last battle against their creator, and they'll either die fighting for their freedom, or survive to live the life they've always yearned for. MM Paranormal Fantasy

(Includes book one from The Valley Ghosts Series, The Consortium Trilogy, and the Stone Series.)

The Ultimate Sacrifice (Four Packs Trilogy Book 2)

https://mybook.to/FourPacksTrilogy

Grady Summerville is facing a slow and agonizing death, but has come to terms with his disease and doesn't fear dying. However, fate has other ideas, presenting him with a future thanks to Max Steele. Grady owes his very life to Max, and as his health improves, finds himself falling head over heels with his savior.

Max Steele has been forced to leave his pack and everyone he knows to move to the West Territory to be a blood donor for Grady. He knows it's the right thing to do, but it doesn't mean he has to like it.

As tensions escalate between the two packs, Max finds his loyalty tested and is torn between following his alpha, or following his heart.

If Max doesn't make the sacrifice then it will be Grady making the ultimate sacrifice and paying with his life.

#MMParanormal #Shifters

A Ghost of a Chance

https://mybook.to/AGhostOfAChance

James McKinney has always lived life alone. He doesn't have a family, at least none that he remembers. He's always dreamed of having a house of his own, a place he can call home. Finding the right house, ready to work to make it his home, nothing can put a damper on his happiness, or can it? Trey Andral, returning home from college, notices someone moving into his old friend's house next door. Miss Hattie is still waving to him from the bedroom window, even though he knows she's gone. He also knows he can't not help the new guy make the house his own. Trey has always been able to see and hear sprits, but what's normal to him is terrifying to most others. When the spirits seem intent on contacting James, Trey has no choice but to share his secret, risking their friendship. If they work together, maybe they can figure out what the clues the spirits are giving them mean. And maybe they can find family in each other.

Tutu (Malicious Gods: Egypt)

https://mybook.to/Tutu

Kit Nelson was thrown into the world of demons and cults as a child. He's learned to depend on no one, and to do all he can to keep himself safe from dark forces. He also knows he can't trust anyone else with his life. He knows what the demons who hunt him have in mind for him, and he'll fight it every step of the way.

Tommy Smythe and his sister Lola have been fighting what they know is a rising tide of evil for years. They're prepared with all their paranormal weaponry, including the assistance of an ancient god who has fought demons his whole existence. Tutu, the Egyptian god and Master of Demons has chosen Tommy to be his vessel and his sword when needed to destroy any and all demons.

A new threat ripples through the dark underworld, one that will be felt across all mankind. A demon has chosen one whose body he will use to return to the land of the living. But only if Kit, Tommy, and Lola can't stop him. Only Tutu has the power and knowledge to protect them from the demon Rerek, and he also knows even with his help, this is not going to be an easy battle.

Amos Ridge

https://mybook.to/AmosRidge

"There's no time. Remember, I love you."It all started with a discovery. A cave beneath a waterfall that held a crystal. Two boys—best friends—embark on a journey they're told will help all mankind. As the years go by, their friendship turns to love, and their adventure turns into a battle.Drew Langly is the keeper of the crystal. With his contact, the crystal allows them to jump to different timestreams and help, if they can, to further that society or fix anything that improves their lives. When he's ripped from the timestream, it's the beginning of what will change everything they've come to know about how the different timestreams function.Colby Adams is Drew's boyfriend, fellow traveler, and jump partner. When Drew is left vulnerable after a failed jump, he's there to help and try to figure out what went wrong. They soon discover another team of travelers is in trouble, but they've been warned against trusting them. The more they learn, the more they realize everything has been a lie. To rewrite a history that's been full of deceit, they'll need to put their trust, once again, in strangers. Can they rewind it all and begin again? Experience the history they were always meant to? With some unconventional help, maybe...

THE THINGS WE LOSE

Chapter One

Griff

Dane slept soundly next to me, Dave the smallest of our three dogs slept as close to my leg as he could on the opposite side, as Flagg and Linny slept on the floor. We'd been living together for more than a year now, and so far, nothing weird had happened that was even close to that day in the warehouse. And I hoped we never experienced anything like that again.

I was no expert in the paranormal, in fact with all the weird shit I'd seen since meeting Dane, it made me want to know even less.

"Why are you still awake?"

"I thought you were asleep."

Dane raised himself off the bed enough to throw his upper body across mine. "I was, but all that thinking you were doing woke me up." Dave huffed out a groan followed by a deep sigh. "See, you even woke up Dave."

"Sorry, guys. I was thinking about how our life has been filled with such strange things. Did you think this would be our reality? Going out looking for ghosts to trap or force to cross over? It's just so strange to think I went from never seeing anything paranormal to seeing more ghosts than I can keep track of." My hand smoothed down his back, and I thought of all the marks he should have had, but for reasons none of us understood, he seemed to still only have the one original mark.

"It is bizarre. We met because we were curious about urban exploring, not ghosts." He snuggled in closer, and I pulled him in tight with a kiss to the top of his head. "Meeting you made it all worth it."

I slept then and neither of us woke up again until my alarm went off. "Don't go yet," he groaned.

"I'm going to shower." I kissed the top of his head as I wiggled away from him and Dave.

Twenty minutes later I was showered and nearly ready for the day. Walking back into the bedroom, I pulled a pair of boxers on before grabbing the jeans I'd worn yesterday.

"Are you busy today?" Dane asked, still tucked under the blankets.

"Yeah, we still have a lot of work to do on that train car they brought in last week." I was a welder by trade and worked mostly on the train cars that moved continuously through the city. An endless supply of work, and frustration.

"Be sure you drink a lot of water it's supposed to be really hot." Dane swung his legs over the bed and hugged me around the waist.

"I will, what are you working on today?" Dane worked from home, and even if I didn't completely understand what he did, I knew he worked hard.

"Oh, same as yesterday. It's a big project so I'll probably be working on it for the next few weeks."

"Let me know if I should bring home dinner." I kissed him once more and headed out the door. Normally we ate breakfast before I left, but today was my day to bring breakfast in to work, and my boss Sid would be waiting for his caffeine.

"Oh, thank god." Sid rushed up to me as soon as I opened the door and took the tray of coffee I held. "I was ready to go into caffeine withdrawal." After checking which coffee was his, he took a big drink before letting out a satisfied groan. "That's what I needed, thanks, Griff."

"Have a donut, it'll fix you right up." I patted his shoulder and walked into the breakroom to set down the box of sugary goodness I'd be helping myself to as soon as I had some coffee.

"We need to try to finish the axle we were working on yesterday. The train waits for no one. I'm pretty sure someone said that before." He squinted one eye and considered his own words before opening the box I'd just set down and taking out a donut.

"I'll get right on it. Dane said it's going to be a hot one today."

"Yeah, we should probably get started and try to be done before it's too miserable. I don't think there's a big enough fan to make it bearable when it's over a hundred and we're welding all day." Sid wrinkled his nose at the thought before taking another big drink of his coffee.

"Alright, let's do this." I shoved a donut in my mouth with one hand while carrying my coffee with the other and kicked open the door to the shop. It was already hot inside, but I ignored it and got busy putting on my gear. We'd worked together for years and had routines that we both stuck to without needing to tell each other.

After putting his leather chaps on, Sid turned to face me before taking a big drink of coffee. "How's Dane doing?"

"He's doing good. Busy with work, and the dogs." I tried not to smile at the mention of his name, but the roll of Sid's eyes told me how very unconvincing I was.

"You two are kinda disgusting you know," He patted me on the back before walking further into the shop.

"Yeah, yeah," I said and neither of us spoke for the next few hours as we worked hard to get the job done. It was so fucking hot I sweated nonstop, and reminded myself to keep drinking water even when I didn't feel like I needed it. We had music playing loud enough to keep me focused on the task at hand, and when I was finally satisfied with what I'd done, I flipped my helmet up.

The relief was instant, as the air from the large industrial fan was finally able to hit my bare skin. I looked over at Sid who was just turning off his welder but had yet to flip up his shield. "Sid?"

"Yeah, what is it?" He threw his head back and his mask lifted enough for him to see me.

"It's fucking hot." Settling my hands on my hips I stood and waited for his reaction.

"What the—get back to work." He threw his head forward and flipped the mask back in place blocking me out.

"I'm done," I cupped my hands and yelled in his direction since he'd turned his back to me.

He spun around to face me, flipped his helmet up, and checked his watch. "Looks like it's time for lunch."

"Did someone say lunch?" Dane stood at the door to the shop holding two bags of food. I had no clue what it was, but I was so happy to see him I had to force myself not to tear my leathers off and scoop him up in my arms.

"Babe, I didn't think you were coming in today." I walked over to him and kissed him soundly while reaching for one of the bags. "What did you bring?"

"Deli sandwiches and a variety of salads and chips. I didn't think you'd want anything hot today, and I knew you'd have a donut for breakfast, so I thought I'd try to balance that out."

"He knows you too well," Sid said as he shed his leathers on the way out of the shop. "Well come on then, let's eat."

He did know me well. Probably better than anyone, and when he looked at me the way he was right now, there wasn't anyone else that would ever take his place in my heart.

"Ready to eat?" he asked, snapping me out of my daydream.

"Yeah, let's go before Sid gets too hangry."

"I heard that," Sid said, making us both laugh.

Chapter Two

Dane

After Griff left for work, I'd tried to keep myself busy with my latest project. But something was bothering me and had been for a while now. The events we'd faced those nights while exploring had been like nothing I'd ever experienced before, and I didn't want to jump back into it without preparing myself as much as I could.

They both took their sandwiches out of one of the bags, a meat combo for Sid, pastrami for Griff, while I had turkey and avocado.

"This is great, thanks, Dane," Sid said with a shake of his sandwich in my direction.

"You're welcome, but I have to make a confession." They both stopped eating to look at me, and Griff put his sandwich down.

"Is everything okay?" he asked.

"Yeah, at least I think it is. I just have this feeling something is coming. Like a sense of foreboding." It sounded weird to my ears, and I knew if Griff didn't love me, he'd be laughing. But instead, he pulled my chair closer to his.

"What's going on?"

"I'm not sure. It's like my skin is charged with electricity. I can't focus enough for work, and I feel like there's something I'm supposed to be preparing for. But I have no clue what."

"Janis did warn us a while back. Have you talked to her?"

"No, not yet. I wasn't sure what to tell her. I haven't had any nightmares, I don't have any premonition of things to come, but I know I should be preparing." It was hard to say out loud, but I knew both of them would understand. After all, they'd both seen what could happen when shit got out of control with the spirit world.

"Let me send her a text," Sid said, and Griff leaned closer to me.

"Are you sure you're okay?" He had so much worry in his eyes, and I hated that I was the one to cause it.

"Yeah. I meant what I said, nothing has happened. I guess I could see if Sophia is feeling any changes from the other side, she's got so much more experience at it than I do."

"Just because she has experience doesn't mean she has understanding."

He'd said this to me many times, and while I knew what he meant, I didn't really comprehend what was behind it. Sophia was the most experienced of us all, and we let her lead us on what to do during an investigation. But lately we had not gone on many of those. "Do you think that's why we haven't been going out on any investigations?"

"That was on me. I didn't want to keep going out on random calls, so I told the others to only gather us all if there was truly a need. I didn't want you to be included if there was a chance you could be harmed," Sid said.

"Did you know about this?" I didn't need to hear Griff's answer to know he was definitely involved. "You know I need to get more experience."

"I know, but so many of the places we go aren't haunted. I thought it was safer to avoid those," Sid explained. "Plus, I don't want to risk you being exposed to the same shit that happened at the old farmhouse. That happened so easy, and you weren't even looking for spirits or anything close to it."

I thought about it for a moment and realized they weren't excluding me, they were protecting me, and that wasn't a bad thing. "Guys, I really do want the experience, so if there's any chance I can have contact with a spirit, please include me."

"Well, I actually wanted to talk to you about that. Do you remember the video where Sophia and the guys explored that old house, and they got the ghost on video?"

"The old man that was laughing at them through the window?"

Sid nodded. "That's the one. We thought it might be a good one to see how we all handle it. I mean we've captured a few spirits and crossed them over, but none of them were as nasty as that one."

Sid was right, that was one of the first videos I'd watched from their team that made me believe ghosts were real, and really creepy. "I think I need to. If we keep avoiding them, I'll never learn how to control whatever it is in me that makes me able to absorb them." It sounded so strange, and it was. But it was a power I wanted to explore and learn to control—not hide away.

"Are you sure?" Griff asked.

"Yeah, but only if you go too."

"There's nothing that would stop me. I think you should go see Janis before we make any plans though. She'll know more about what to expect and how to deal with it."

"Sorry to interrupt, Janis replied and said to get your butts over there. She's been patiently waiting for you to call or visit and is disappointed it's taken you this long. Her words not mine," Sid said, and cleared his throat. "We're pretty much done for the day and it's too hot to work much longer. You two go ahead, and I'll clean up the shop."

"Are you sure? I think Janis might like a chance to say hello to you," Griff teased.

"Oh, I'm sure. I can only handle one visit per year, and after what she told us last time, I'm good for a while."

Sid and Griff were both creeped out by Janis, but to me she was very sweet and caring. She had a weird vibe of someone who knew too much but chose to only share a tiny amount. Maybe that was the exact reason they both avoided her, she knew too much from the other side of the veil.

Neither Sid nor Griff were big believers in the paranormal, but now they'd both seen enough to know it was real whether they chose to believe or not. After what had happened to me, I had no doubt it was real. Griff washed up before checking with Sid that he really was alright with cleaning up alone.

"Get going," Sid yelled from the back just as Griff walked out of the shop area.

"You heard him, let's go." Griff and I walked out the back door and right over to his car. "I'll drive." We both got in and sat a moment while the air conditioner cooled it down.

"I'm not sure Janis can really help me, it feels like I'm wasting her time."

"She would never tell you no if you needed help, and right now you *need help*." Griff took my hand and rubbed the back of it with his thumb. "It's okay, and if she thinks you don't need her right now, she'll give you some advice on how to calm the feelings you're having."

He was right, and eventually I hoped to feel the same confidence in myself that he had in me.

Chapter Three

Griff

Dane was worried, and even though he tried to hide it, I knew if he'd felt the need to drive over to my work in the middle of a heatwave, he did it for a reason. I reached for his hand and squeezed it, bringing his attention back from where he'd been staring out the side window. "Everything okay?"

"Yeah, I just can't shake this weird feeling. It's so frustrating. I can't put a name to exactly how I feel, or why I know to prepare for whatever is coming, but I just do."

"I think you'll understand more when you talk to Janis." He'd been speaking with her occasionally, but I think he'd hoped to avoid anything too serious in dealing with the other side of the veil. But now it seemed he'd have no choice in that. She did say he'd been chosen.

"What do you think of Sid's suggestion to go to that old house?"

"I'm not sure. I don't want you to ever be put in the situation you were in at that warehouse, or at the farmhouse. It was all horrible, and I hated there was nothing I could do to help." Remembering his face when he was possessed, and how his features had changed from someone who was happy and carefree to a creature I barely recognized, scared me. I didn't want him to go through that ever again, and I knew I wouldn't be able to stand back and let it happen. Even if he could absorb a spirit, I wasn't willing to test that theory with his life.

"Maybe that's what I'm meant to do? I don't know how much I believe about me being the one who can bear the marks and will be the one that saves everyone. It's a lot to live up to, especially when I don't have any clue how I would do that."

It was the first time he'd said that. Normally he'd either brush off Janis's prediction, or he'd ignore it and try to change the subject. I wasn't sure he believed it, and if I was being honest with myself, I hoped it was wrong. "Let's see what she says. Have you heard from those other guys we met last year?"

"The ones that can speak to the dead? No. I was going to call, and I know I was supposed to, but it's just disturbing. And not to be rude but they're both a little different."

I grinned and tried not to laugh. Dane never met anyone he didn't like, but I had to admit there was a weird feeling around those two that made it hard to relax around them. The ghost hunters we'd met were different. I knew some of them possessed paranormal skills, but they were all regular guys with powers they used to help ghosts or eliminate them, depending on the nature of the haunting. "What do you think of the ghost hunters?" I had to ask.

"They seem nice enough, one of them called me. Jason, I think it was. But I haven't gotten back to any of them." He stared at Janis's house as we pulled up out front, and I noticed there were a few extra cars parked nearby.

I turned the car off and twisted to face him. "You don't have to do any of this if you don't want to. I know it's not your choice, and if you want nothing more to do with it then we can leave now, and I'll tell them we're out. It's all up to you."

He looked down at his hands in his lap and I knew he was mulling over his choices. It was always obvious to me that neither of us had grown more accustomed to the paranormal, or the supernatural. It was all just as foreign to us now as it had been when we'd walked into that warehouse. But now we had each other, and I'd burn down the world to keep him safe. "I want to go in and see what they say. I have a feeling it's not just Janis inside. But I know they're all concerned about the predictions they see and want to plan for it. I can give them my time at least."

"Then that's what we'll do." I got out of the car and met him on the sidewalk. We walked hand in hand, and when Janis opened the door before we were close enough for her to know we were there, neither of us were shocked this time.

"Come in, boys. Everyone is here. I know you're having some doubts about your involvement with our little motley crew, and I want you to know we all understand. Each of us has different reasons for being in our group, and I know you must feel like your choice has been taken away. Dane, if you don't think you want to be involved you can leave now, and we'll never bother you again. But I suspect a part of you is trying to warn you that something is coming." Janis spoke softly and spared no words as she led us to the back of her house. There on her patio were all the people we'd met previously. The two guys from the morgue sat at the far end of the group and seemed somehow separate from everyone else. The ghost hunters were all together with Sophia across from them.

"Hey, Dane, how have you been?" Jason stood and walked over to us, and after shaking both our hands led us to where everyone else was gathered. "I know this is unusual. But please, give us a chance."

Dane hesitated before he answered. I stayed quiet. Anything we did was his choice, not mine. "I want to stay, but I'm still not sure how I can help."

"We're all going to talk about what our roles are in this strange situation we find ourselves in," Janis said. "Bran, why don't you start."

Bran's eyes widened before he stood to speak. "So, you all know Jordan and I work at the morgue. Well, after our last meeting things have only gotten stranger. There used to be spirits that would wander in with the dead on a regular basis. They were confused, or maybe even angry, but all of them had the same two things in common. They either wanted to cross over to their loved ones, or they wanted revenge on someone who was still living and were willing to hang around to do that. I don't deal with those spirits, they're just nasty and you cannot reason with them." The other guy, Jordan, next to him, snickered, but Bran ignored him and kept talking.

"Lately, there are no spirits coming in with any of the dead we've received. It's been this way for months, and I'm not gonna lie, at first, I was thrilled. But then I remembered how my mother collected spirits and used them to do her bidding. I don't know if that's what's happening now, or if it's what was predicted beginning to happen, but whatever it is there is something happening in the spirit world."

He sat down and fought a smile as Jordan leaned against him. I had to admit even though they were weird, they were also very cute. Both had dark hair and pale skin probably from being inside way too much. Jordan's hair was all over the place and looked like it was probably never under control while Bran's was cut short and neat.

"I've felt something lately that I can't explain," Dane surprised me by saying. "It feels like there's electricity under my skin, and there's something I need to be preparing for but I'm not sure what that is. It's all confusing and overwhelming at the same time." He looked so lost and hopeless that I couldn't stop myself from pulling him onto my lap. "I'm not sure how else to describe it."

"I've been feeling the same," Sophia, the girl that had the same markings as Dane, said. If I had to guess I'd say she had even more marks now, but I had only seen her a few times, and I tried not to stare at her when we did get together. Her markings were strange like Dane's, they were visible when there was a spirit or demon near, and glowed when they were needed, but most of the time they were invisible. "My marks are visible all the time lately. I'm not sure why. For months they were hidden but everyday another seems to appear." She held her arms out and twisted them around showing us how her marks were now all so close together it was hard to tell where one ended and another began.

"Is the feeling I have related to the prophecy?" Dane asked.

"I'm not sure," Janis said after a moment. "The spirit world has been filled with lots of static lately. It makes it hard for me to focus on any one thought to know what's going on, or what can be. It's like there's someone trying to block the signal they send to me."

"Has that ever happened before?" her brother asked. He sat at the other end of the patio with his arms crossed looking as pissed off as he always did while his husband sat next to him taking in every word.

"No, not like this. There have been attempts from this side to block the signal we psychics have that connects us to the other side, but nothing close to this."

"Like electricity under your skin," Wade, Jason's husband, mumbled from next to him.

"What if the two are connected? Maybe they're using other people with a connection to the other side, to block the signal from getting through?" Everyone gasped at Dane's suggestion and looked from person to person hoping for answers.

"I was afraid to consider that," Janis said. "Dane, tell us more."

Thanks for reading! I hope you check out the first book The Things We Find to see where it all begins.

Mystical Markings

The Things We Lose Book Two: https://mybook.to/TTWLose

Book One: The Things We Find: https://mybook.to/TheThingsWeFIND